# Spo

# A

# The Tennis Ball

***Spotty Cat Bedtime Series***



**Mark Warren**

## Acknowledgements

I would like to acknowledge the real creative ones:
my boys, Tor and Casper,
and,
my wife, Britt.

## About the Author

Mark Warren creates imaginative and heartwarming books for children aged three to eight years old. He is passionate about fostering curiosity, values, and kindness in children through stories that blend entertainment with valuable life lessons. His books also aim to create a cosy environment — calming children before bed.

When not writing, he enjoys sharing the outdoor life with his young family, who inspire many of his memorable characters.

Spotty Cat was snuggling with Mummy Cat, Daddy Cat, Black Cat with White Feet, and White Cat with Black Feet — all warm in their cosy bed.

Spotty Cat woke up with a paw on his head and a tail on his nose. He had no idea which way was up — or which way was down — but he knew it was time to get up.

He clambered his way out and sat on the edge of the big bed.

“Mummy Cat... Mummy Cat... wake up, Mummy Cat,” meowed Spotty Cat, tapping Mummy Cat’s head with his soft paw.

“Good morning, Spotty Cat,” meowed back Mummy Cat in a very sleepy voice.

“Mummy Cat... Mummy Cat... Mummy Cat... what are we doing today?” asked Spotty Cat.

“Well, I’m going back to sleep,” said Mummy Cat. “You can go and play — but be back for lunch!”

Spotty Cat went downstairs, had some breakfast, brushed his teeth — and, as it was a warm spring morning, he decided to go and play in the forest next to his house.

After Spotty Cat had scampered about in the forest, looking unsuccessfully for animals to chase, he spotted something moving out of the corner of his eye.

*Maybe something to chase at last,* he thought.

Spotty Cat crouched down — and as he got closer, he could see triangular ears, daring eyes, a little black nose, rather sharp teeth, strong paws, a fast-wagging tail — and something else that looked like a yellow tennis ball!

Spotty Cat sneaked further — and as he got closer, he realised it wasn't a tennis ball, but a little round yellow bird. And the triangular ears belonged to a young wolf!

Spotty Cat peered out from behind a tree, listening intently.
"Please don't eat me," begged the little round yellow bird.
"I wanted to eat you," murmured the wolf,
"but you're too cute to eat!"
It was true — the little yellow bird had huge round eyes,
tiny little feet, and a body like a fluffy ball.
"Thank goodness for that, nice wolf," said the little bird.
"I would rather be your friend than your breakfast!"
After a pause, the wolf said, "I don't really have any friends
— everyone is afraid of me."
The little round yellow bird looked at the wolf with his big
eyes, hopped up onto the wolf's back, and chirped, "Well, I
want to be your first friend."

As Spotty Cat tried to get a little closer, a twig snapped under his paw, which made the wolf and the little bird look around at him.

"Err... hi there!" meowed Spotty Cat in a rather nervous voice, not knowing what else to say.

"Hello," chirped the little round bird.

"Hey," greeted the wolf in a friendly tone.

"My name is Spotty Cat," said Spotty Cat as he introduced himself and asked about them. "What's your name?"

"My name is Wolfie," answered the wolf.

"My name is Budgeri," sweetly replied the little round yellow bird.

“Well, nice wolf, do you like eating cats?” Spotty Cat hesitantly asked.

“No,” chuckled Wolfie, “they taste like rotten mice.”

“That’s good to know,” said Spotty Cat with a relieved sigh, as he cautiously walked over to both of them.

The new trio found they had a lot in common: they lived on the same road, loved adventure and playing in the woods — but also wanted others to play with. Spotty Cat suggested they all come for lunch at his house, and they agreed.

On the way to Spotty Cat's house, it was not clear if Budgeri could really fly — it was more of a floating bounce. Her little wings flapped very quickly, but not effectively, and occasionally she crashed into a tree or a bush — though she acted as if it was completely normal. Wolfie, on the other hand, was clearly a master of the forest, just like Spotty Cat — flying over obstacles with ease.

"Here we are!" announced Spotty Cat as they reached his front door. "Mummy Cat, Daddy Cat — I'm home. Is there enough lunch for my new friends?"

Mummy Cat came out of the kitchen and froze. The hair on her arched back was sticking up, and her wide eyes jumped between the wolf and the bird at her front door.

"It's okay, Mummy Cat," said Spotty Cat. "These are my new friends — Wolfie and Budgeri."

After what seemed like a whole minute, Mummy Cat said, "Most birds in this house are for eating, and most wolves want to eat us! Daddy Cat... come here."

Daddy Cat had a similar reaction — a bird too cute to eat, and a wolf who, even though he seemed friendly, still had very sharp teeth.

"Well," Mummy Cat began again cautiously, "there is enough lunch for everyone."

After Black Cat with White Feet and White Cat with Black Feet got over their initial shock, they all sat down for a lovely lunch together — and instantly warmed to Budgeri and Wolfie.

“Never judge a book by its cover,” remarked Spotty Cat.

“Very true,” agreed Daddy Cat.

After Spotty Cat's new friends had gone home, the family was so tired and sleepy that they decided it was time for a nap.

They all snuggled into their cosy bed — heads, feet, tails, and paws everywhere — and fell asleep, dreaming of new adventures.

Made in the USA
Middletown, DE
09 June 2025

76743758R00020